W9-ASF-301

For Isabelle

– J.E.

In loving memory of my
wonderful mum, Tanya

XXX

– R.H.

LIBRARY OF CONGRESS CATALOGING-IN-PUBLICATION DATA
Emmett, Jonathan.
Ruby in her own time / by Jonathan Emmett; illustrated by Rebecca Harry.– 1st American ed. p. cm.
Summary: Ruby, the last of Mother Duck's and Father Duck's eggs to hatch, is slower to develop
than her four siblings, until the day that she flies farther and higher than any of them.
ISBN 0-439-57915-5 (alk. paper)
[1. Growth–Fiction. 2. Individuality–Fiction. 3. Ducks–Fiction.] I. Harry, Rebecca, ill.
II. Title. PZ7.E696 On 2004 [E]–dc21 2003008464

10 9 8 7 6 5 4 3 2 1 04 05 06 07 08
Printed in Belgium

First American edition, February 2004

RUBY in Her Own Time

Written by
Jonathan Emmett

Illustrated by
Rebecca Harry

SCHOLASTIC PRESS • NEW YORK

Once upon a time
upon a nest
beside a lake,
there lived two ducks –

a mother duck
and
a father duck.

There were five eggs in the nest. Mother Duck sat upon the nest,

all day...

and all night...

through howling wind . . .

and driving rain,
looking after
the eggs –
ALL five of them.

Then, one bright morning,
the eggs began to hatch.

One

two

three

four

little beaks poked out
into the sunlight.

One

two

three

four

little ducklings shook their feathers in the breeze.

“We’ll call them Rufus, Rory, Rosie, and Rebecca,” said Father Duck. And Mother Duck agreed.

But the fifth egg did **nothing.**

"Will it **ever** hatch?"
said Father Duck.

"It will," said
Mother Duck,
"in its own time."

And –

sure enough –

it did.

"She's very small,"
said Father Duck.
"What shall we call her?"

"We'll call her Ruby,"
said Mother Duck,
"because she's small
and precious."

Rufus, Rory, Rosie, and Rebecca
ate whatever they were given.

They ate anything and
everything.

But Ruby ate
nothing.

"Will she **ever** eat?"
said Father Duck.

"She will," said Mother Duck,
"in her own time."

And –

sure enough –

she did.

Rufus, Rory, Rosie, and Rebecca
swam off whenever they were able.

They swam anywhere
and everywhere.
But Ruby swam nowhere.

"Will she ever swim?"
said Father Duck.
"She will," said Mother Duck,
"in her own time."

And –
sure enough –
she did.

Rufus, Rory, Rosie, and Rebecca
grew **bigger.**

And Ruby grew **bigger** too. Her feathers grew out, and her wings grew broad and beautiful.

And when Rufus, Rory, Rosie, and Rebecca began to fly...

. . . Ruby flew too!

Rufus, Rory, Rosie,
and Rebecca flew far
and wide. They flew out
across the water.
They flew up among
the trees.

But Ruby flew farther and wider.
She flew out **beyond** the water.

She flew up **above** the trees.
She flew anywhere and **everywhere**.

She stretched out her
beautiful wings . . .

and soared **high**
among the clouds.

Mother Duck and Father Duck
watched Ruby flying off into the distance.

"Will she ever come back?"
said Mother Duck.
"She will," said Father Duck,
"in her own time."

And –
sure enough –
SHE DID.